Story by
Gina Bittner

Illustrated by
Kelly Kingsley

How
Rudy
the
Rooster
Got His Voice

Handersen Publishing, LLC
Lincoln, Nebraska USA

Handersen Publishing, LLC
Lincoln, Nebraska

How Rudy the Rooster Got His Voice

Manufactured in the United States of America.

Summary: Rudy the Rooster doesn't sound like the other roosters on the farm. By asking a few animal friends, he finds his voice and discovers it's okay to be just the way you are.

Library of Congress Control Number: 2019933462
Handersen Publishing, LLC, Lincoln, Nebraska

Paperback ISBN: 978-1-947854-64-2
Hardback ISBN: 978-1-947854-65-9
eBook ISBN: 978-1-947854-66-6

Publisher Website: www.handersenpublishing.com
Publisher Email: editors@handersenpublishing.com

Dedicated to all creatures everywhere who were faced with a challenge, yet persevered.

Baaawk-a-doodle-doo!

Baaawk-a-doodle-doo!

Baaawk-a-doodle-doo!

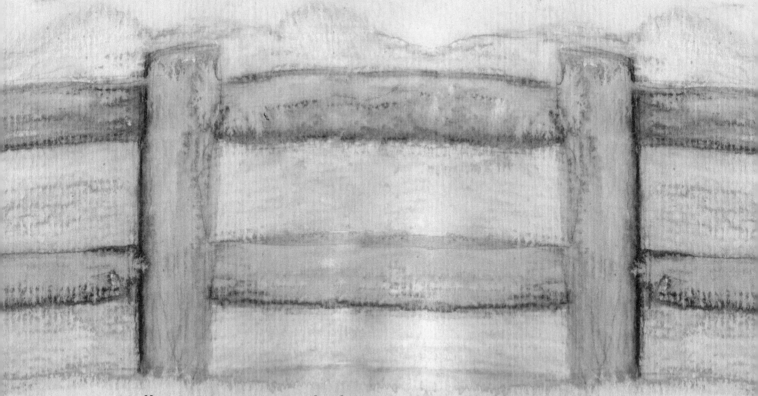

Hello! My name is Rudy the Rooster, and I love sharing my voice. When I was a young rooster, I had trouble figuring out how I should sound. At first, it came out like this...

No matter how much I practiced...

At 6:00 a.m.

GLUUUUCCCCKKKK!

At 6:00 p.m.

GLUUUUCCCCKKKK!

At 2:00 a.m.

GLUUUUCCCCKKKK!

It always came out all wrong.

I was kept in a pen with another rooster and two hens.
Surely that meant I was a chicken too, didn't it?
But why did my pal Roadie the Rooster sound NORMAL?

Baaawk
-a-doodle-
-doo!!!

What was wrong with me? Am I broken? Just shy?
AM I EVEN A ROOSTER?

But I still made a sound like this...

GLUUUUCCCCKKKK!

GLUUUUCCCCKKKK!

GLUUUUCCCCKKKK!

At 6:00 a.m.

GLUUUUCCCCKKKK!

At 6:00 p.m.

GLUUUUCCCCKKKK!

At 2:00 a.m.

GLUUUUCCCCKKKK!

It always came out all wrong.

I kept right on practicing, morning, noon, and night. But still, it always came out all wrong. Maybe the other farm animals could help me. Off I went to find my friends.

"Hello there, Mrs. Cow! Can you help me?" I asked my black-and-white friend.

GLUUUUCCCCKKKK!

"What's your moo-lemma, Rudy?" asked Mrs. Cow.

GLUUUUCCCCKKKK!

"I have been trying to sound like my friend Roadie the Rooster," I told her. "He's a rooster like me. But every time I try, it always comes out all wrong."

GLUUUUCCCCKKKK!

"Pardon me, Mr. Ruffy and Miss Kitty," I said. "But do you think you could listen to something for me? I've been to see Mrs. Cow, and Squealers, but they couldn't help me. Maybe you can?"

GLUUUUCCCCKKKK-a-ooooo!

"Wait! Did you hear that?" I exclaimed. "Let me try that again..."

GLUUUUCCCCKKKK-a-ooooo!

hank you, friends!" I said. "You've been so much help."

"That sure is a problem," said Mrs. Cow. "But you better moo-ve along to someone who can help."

"Oink! What's going on, Rudy?" asked Squealers the Pig. "Have you gotten mud in your feathers again?"

"Not today, Squealers," I said. "But I do have a problem that I hope you can help me with. Listen to this..."

GLUUUUCCCCKKKK!

"Do you notice how WRONG that is?" I asked. "I don't sound like a rooster at all! And no matter how much I practice, it always comes out all wrong."

GLUUUUCCCCKKKK!

"You surely are in a mucky situation," said Squealers. "But it's time for my mud bath, so I can't help you."

"Purrrr-fect," said Miss Kitty. "But I'm not sure what we did."
"Woof," agreed Mr. Ruffy.

I used my voice! I used it, and used it, and used it. Finally, I started to sound more like the rooster I knew I was. As I grew older, I became better at using my voice.

GLUUUUCCCCKkkk-a-google-goo!

GLUUUUCCCCKKKK-a-google-goo!

GLUUUUCCCCKKKK-a-google-GOO!

The hens started laying eggs right there in our chicken coop.
I'm definitely a rooster! And I'm right where I belong.
I still used my voice all the time. But you know what?
My voice started to change on me all over again!

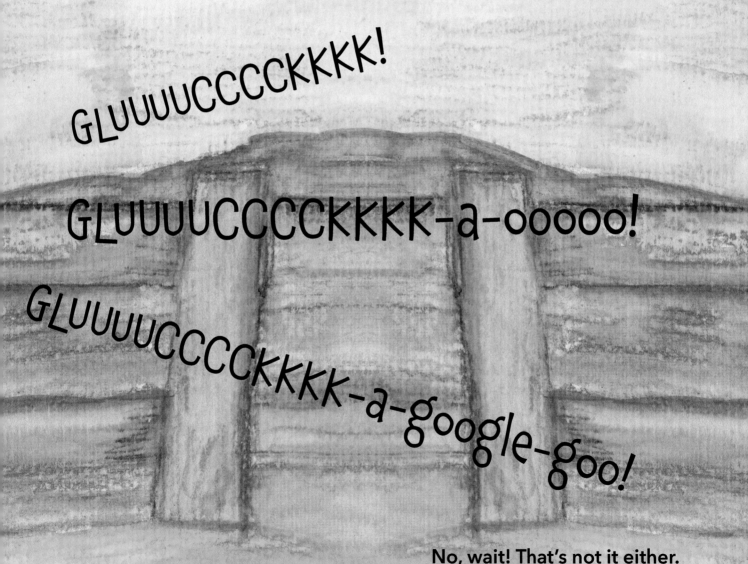

GLUUUCCCCKKKK!

GLUUUUCCCCKKKK-a-ooooo!

GLUUUUCCCCKKKK-a-google-goo!

No, wait! That's not it either.

Well, I kept on using my voice, all day and all night. I was so proud of my voice. But I knew I needed to keep on practicing, so I did! Now my voice sounds more like this...

At 6:00 a.m.

Baaawk-a-doodle-doo!

At 6:00 p.m.

Baaawk-a-doodle-doo!

At 2:00 a.m.

Baaawk-a-doodle-DOO!

Remember, no matter who you are, or what your challenges are...
DON'T GIVE UP!

Take it from me—just keep practicing! And you know what? If it doesn't come out quite right the first time, that's okay!

Because it's just who YOU are.

Baaawk-a-doodle-doo!
Baaawk-a-doodle-doo!
Baaawk-a-doodle-doo!

And YOU are special just by being...

baaawk-a-doodle-
YOU!!!

Dr. Gina Bittner is a first-time author who has used her 21 years of teaching to inspire her ideas and keep her creativity alive. Between teaching special education, elementary education, being a college professor, and a mom and foster mom, the ideas are endless and she cannot wait to put them all on paper! For the past 12 years and counting, Gina has been a college professor at Peru State College where she primarily teaches elementary reading and math methods, children's literature, and reading interventions. Gina's hobbies include farm living (that's a hobby, right?), camping, crafting, baking, and living vicariously through her children's endeavors.

Kelly Kingsley has been drawing since she could hold a writing utensil. You will find her painting with watercolor, sketching, decorating cookies with royal icing, and painting pet portraits in her free time. Kelly has been an educator for 30 years and counting. She spent 26 of those years teaching elementary school and is now an assistant professor of education at Peru State College in Nebraska. She enjoys lake living with her husband, and has two married daughters who are also educators. A new grandson joined the family this summer, so reading books and babysitting are keeping her busy.

Rudy the Rooster found his voice!
And you can too!

5 tips for finding your voice:

- Be Yourself.

- Keep practicing.

- Ask for help.

- Be kind.

- Make your own noise.

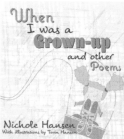

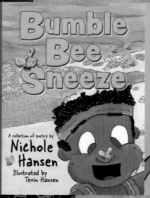
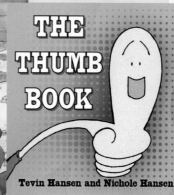

Handersen Publishing LLC
Great books for young readers
www.handersenpublishing.com

Made in the USA
Columbia, SC
19 March 2019

City of Melissa
3411 Barker Avenue
Melissa, TX   54